"The stories in this collection by Fran Lewis are gripping in suspense and demonstrate a vivid imagination. I picked them up planning to read for a few minutes and couldn't stop until I had finished the last story. Fran understands well and expresses the dark side that many people have. Motivated by greed or self-interest, some in these stories who seem like people we encounter every day are willing to undertake terrifying actions. It makes for an excellent read."

— Allan Topol, author of *The Italian Divide* and *The Washington Lawyer*

"Hidden Truths and Lies is a compilation of stories told from beyond the grave each one filled with terror as the character faces his or her own fate. The final two stories are pure science fiction and will hopefully allow readers to see the magnitude of this talented writer."

— Susan Ross, Board Of Education, NYC

"Multi-dimensional collection of seven stories that offers a creepy perspective from the viewpoint of the dead and buried. Almost a slice of life, Fran Lewis has a wonderful flair for capturing the essence of her characters and tells the story leading up to their untimely demise. Macabre and deliberately vague, her descriptive narrative captures the paranoia, angst, anger, and indignation of each victim with in-depth characterizations wonderfully plotted leaving the reader eager to turn the page. There is more to this book that meet the eye, and it makes for excellent discussions of people and their choices. Complex, suitably scary with a pinch of cozy realism, this book will leave you making sure you locked the door at night."

— Carole Roman, Amazon reviewer

Hidden Truths & Lies

FRAN LEWIS
WITH CONTRIBUTION BY **JAKE SWERDLOFF**

PUBLISHED BY FIDELI PUBLISHING, INC.

ISBN: 978-1-60414-912-8

Stories

27 minutes: Silenced.. 1

The Betrayal...31

The Imposters...37

The Competitor...44

Journey to Nowhere 57

Crime Pays Off: Just Don't Get Caught 73

Dedications

A special dedication to the memory of my mom, Ruth Swerdloff. She was the inspiration behind my reading and loving the power of words, always encouraging me to read at least five or six books a week. Taking notes on each one helped me as a book reviewer and author today.

A special thank you to Tony Fata, my hairdresser, and Maria D., for allowing me to use them as the main characters in my book, as well as Florio, who gave me the inspiration for the detective in this book.

Another special thank you to my nephew, Jake Swerdloff, for co-authoring "The Competitor" with me, and guiding me through the process of understanding baseball better.

Thank you to Maxine Bringenberg for editing my book and keeping me on target and on point. You are the best.

Acknowledgments

To my sister MJ (Marcia Joyce): your spirit guides me every single day, and your memory will be in my heart and soul forever. Without your dare to review my first book, I don't think I would have had the nerve to become an author, book reviewer, and talk show host. Thanks to you and our antics when we were kids, the Bertha Series keeps your memory alive.

Thank you to my cousin, Susan Ross, for always being there when I need someone to read my work before it's published, and for just being my best friend ever.

Thank you to my husband, Jeff Lewis, who is my rock, my special love, and who is always there for me.

Introduction

Each story in this series teaches a lesson the person behind the stone should have learned before committing crime, hurting someone else, or generally failing at life. We're about to enter Golden Stone Cemetery, where these unfortunate people are buried so deep you can barely find their markers. Their crimes are so heinous and their deeds so cruel that family members buried them here because they want to forget they ever existed.

Welcome to Golden Stone Cemetery, where the voices of these unfortunates can be heard loud and clear. Learning what they did and what their fates became will make you shudder. When you find out just how cruel they were in life, you'll be glad they're gone. You'll be relieved that their families made sure the spirits of each of these nefarious characters will never rise again.

Who lies behind these unmarked stones? Let their stories unfold…

27 Minutes: Silenced

Traumatic brain injuries are common. They can be caused by not wearing a seatbelt while riding in a car, biking without a helmet, falling headfirst down the stairs, or just hitting your head really hard. Falling over and hitting your head on a tabletop or against a sharp edge on the wall might garner the same result.

Maria's Prologue:

Six feet under and nowhere to go. The air is musty and the accommodations crowded. There is no one to hear my screams or to feel my pain. If you are reading this you know it's too late for me. Read my story and decide: was my death from natural causes or murder?

My name is Maria and I was blindsided by love. I thought the man I married and knew for over 25 years really cared about me…

PART I

Prelude to Death

Marriage is supposed to be a partnership, where two people worked for the common goal of making each other happy. Well, I can tell you, that's a crock of you know what!

Tony and I met at Starbucks. He had a mocha latte and I had hot chocolate with whipped cream. Romantic, right? Tony made the first move and asked if we could spend our fifteen minutes of coffee time, or in my case hot chocolate time, together. Thinking it would be nice to talk with someone instead of sitting alone, I readily accepted his invitation and sealed my fate. Tony told me about his ex-wife, Sarah and his two children, Annabelle and Eva. I told him about my two children as well.

I realized as he talked about his girls that Annabelle was his favorite and could do no wrong in his opinion. Eva, on the other hand, was a total failure in his eyes. I'd met his ex-wife before. She was the type who spent most of her days listening to her own voice, giving what she thought was sage advice to anyone who would listen. I knew she was hoping to get a huge divorce settlement from Tony, claiming she was entitled to it for staying married to him for so long.

Tony and I ended up going out to dinner that Saturday. We had a great evening and got to know each other better. I told him about being managing partner of the law firm where I worked, and he said he owned a small but profitable pharmacy.

Several weeks later, he suggested I meet his two daughters. The meeting didn't go well and I should've seen the red flags waving then, but I ignored them. The girls were cold, calculating, and nasty, asking him for money on the spot, like they planned just to see my reaction. They also talked incessantly about their mother, and trying to make me feel uncomfortable. They succeeded.

Despite the less than stellar meeting with his daughters, I continued seeing Tony. One thing led to another, and before too long Tony and I tied the knot.

Fast forward to the present. We've been together for 25 years now. Lately, Tony's temper had been rising and he had been coming home late. The SOB even had the nerve to expect dinner on the table as soon as he sauntered in, even though he'd never called to let me know when he'd be home.

He always smelled of perfume and was covered in red lipstick on these occasions. His explanation was that he'd several meetings and everyone liked to give him warm greetings. This particular night, I asked what else they liked to give, and he shrugged it off as if it were no big deal.

Going to bed angry, I decided to sleep on the couch in the living room so I didn't have to deal with him all night. If he got any more insufferable I might have to buy another bed just to have a place to escape from him.

The next morning, I had a weird feeling from the minute I got up, but couldn't put my finger on it. I thought maybe I was being paranoid. It didn't help that I'd heard Tony whispering to someone on his cell phone, and quickly closed down the conversation when I entered the room.

I'd always thought I was happily married. I was beginning to think I was wrong. I'd never cheated on Tony, but I wasn't sure he was that loyal to me. He made lots of out of town trips, and I wasn't sure they were really for business.

Then there was his assistant, Rosalina. She looked more like a hoochie-coochie mama than a pharmacy assistant. I didn't think she was into learning anything about her job; I thought she was into something else, if you get my drift.

I consoled myself with the thought that every woman likes to think men are interested them, so smiling, flirting with another man, and going for coffee after work was totally innocent. Right? Tony was tall and handsome, with dark hair and bedroom eyes, and women were constantly coming on to him, even when I was with him.

On the other hand, I was no dog. I was thin and fairly attractive, with straight, blonde hair. I always dressed well and wore nothing but designer fashions. Even though I was 65 and a great-grandmother, I was a fit and could still pass for under forty. I loved life, and had every reason to live and enjoy it.

Tony always worked so many hours, that sometimes I was lonely. He indulged my every whim, but then threw it back in my face that the Platinum Card was in his name and he could cut it off at any time, just to humiliate me. Maybe letting me spend his money was his way of eliminating his guilt.

Tony and I had our usual Monday morning discussion about finances, his self-worth and my lack of it. His condescending attitude always started my week off with a big fat sour note. He gave me his usual lecture about how hard he had to work to pay for all of my bills.

After listening to his tirade for over twenty minutes, I put on my coat and decided to leave before the heart palpitations I was feeling got worse. I knew that my blood pressure was rising because I was feeling lightheaded, but would never let Tony know he'd gotten to me like this. I headed to my exercise class to work off some of this stress.

As I pulled out of the lot at my complex, I began to feel more relaxed. Watching Tony drive off in the opposite direction helped too. I shut off my cell phone so I wouldn't have to listen to him if he decided to call and continue his diatribe while I was driving. I turned the volume up on my car radio and entered the line of traffic on the Palisades Parkway on my way to my exercise class.

I met my friend at the class and had a great workout. I felt invigorated and at least five pounds thinner by the end of the session. I thought my day was looking up. Little did I know…

After class, I decided to firm up my plans for the weekend by calling for tickets to a new Broadway show, and then doing some quick food shopping. Plus, I planned to stop at my favorite boutique to buy some clothes before heading to the office.

I was a managing partner in the Louis Fata law firm. I enjoyed working with Mark, Joseph, and Michelle, the paralegal that did much of the research and worked late hours along with the rest of us. Mark and Joseph were lawyers with the firm, but were not partners. I loved what I did, but lately there had been so many changes that I dreaded going into work to find out whose hours I had to cut, who would be laid off. Before I even took off my jacket and had my morning coffee, I knew I'd have unpleasantness waiting for me at ever turn.

When I got to the office that day, I began feeling a heaviness in my chest. I thought it might be indigestion from the waffles and eggs I'd for breakfast. I got settled in my office, then met with my legal team. I even remembered to send someone to the bank to make the weekly deposits so we could make the payroll — it was Friday after all.

Once my meeting was done, I decided to work on some briefs, type up some depositions, and get a jump on some of the things I needed to deal with the next week.

When I went out for lunch, I had the feeling I was being followed. I went into the lot of a McDonalds to get a hot chocolate, and a red car pulled up right next to me. When I pulled out, the red car followed me, not even hiding the fact that it was tailing me.

I tried to see the driver as I looked at the vehicle in my rearview mirror, but the person was wearing a hat that covered his/her entire face. All I could see were intent eyes staring at me. I had a cold chill and worried that someone was out to get me, but had no idea why.

I had secrets I didn't want revealed. But so what? Everyone has secrets, don't they?

Walking into the office, I checked to see if that car had parked in the lot. There was no sign of it, but I still had an uneasy feeling.

I wasn't going to say anything about the incident to anyone at work, but Aggie noticed something was wrong as soon as I walked through the door.

"Maria, what's bothering you? You look like you just saw a ghost."

"Everything's fine. Thanks for asking, though." I never liked to mix work with my personal life, but maybe if I had told her the outcome would have been different.

I spent the rest of the day going through the motions with my clients and reading the briefs for an upcoming trial. I never noticed a tall, dark gentlemen lurking in the corner of the reception area until I heard Agnes ask if she could help him. He didn't answer, just glared and left.

Chills ran down my spine. I hadn't seen the face of the driver following me, but something told me the guy who'd just left had something to do with it. Who was this creepy man and why did he follow me?

Agnes followed her instincts and was out the door quickly to see where he went. When she came back in, she said she couldn't find him anywhere.

The rest of the day I felt a little off balance and tense. I was sure others could see it in my face and the twitch in my eye as well as my shaking hands. I tried to think of anyone who would want to intimidate or hurt me. A horrific thought crept into my head. Could it be her? How would she have found me? I hadn't seen her for over 25 years. Could she still be out for revenge? If it was her, then who was the man? Maybe she hired someone to off me.

My secret past could not come out. If this was her, someone else had done the work of finding me. She was too stupid to find her way across the street. I decided to make a phone call to someone I hadn't spoken to in many years. Could she be working with him? I never thought she would double cross me.

I kept trying to think back to how this might've started. My best friend, Audrey Ross, was the only one that knew the truth about me and who I really was. I'd changed my name, my appearance, and even got a new Social Security number so that no one would ever find me. The Witness Protection Program swore that all traces of my past would be erased. They even moved my kids from my first marriage and didn't tell me where they were — all so they'd be protected.

So, who was following me and why? Were they trying to make sure that I remained silent? Did Audrey give away my identity, or was it someone in the law office working both sides of the fence?

The only person in my life who might be evil enough to come after me was Eve. A malicious bitch, no one wanted to mess with her, including the clients. She was a cop who worked for us part time, and always wore a gun strapped to her ankle at work.

I picked up my cell and dialed Audrey's number, hoping she would answer the phone and not her husband Noel.

"What's up, Maria? What's going on?"

"Audrey, are you alone? Can you talk? I am in deep trouble. I think my past is about to intrude on my present. I'm so stressed out about it that I'm about to keel over. I've got high blood pressure, you know. I'm having palpitations as we speak. I'm totally terrified; my hands are sweating and the rest of me is ice cold."

"Calm down, Maria. Don't be so paranoid."

"I'm afraid she knows."

"How could she know where you are? Who could've told her?"

As I was talking to Audrey, I sensed someone else is in the room with her and I heard a low whisper. Apparently she had me on speakerphone, and someone was listening to our conversation. Instead of answering her, I hung up and hoped she wasn't taping the call. I couldn't believe she would double cross me. I was supposed to be her best friend. It must have something to do with Noel.

Audrey and I had gone to law school together and hoped to work together in the same firm after graduation. We had fun going to classes, doing our assignments, and going shopping in the city after our classes. Audrey and I had been best friends forever. She knew everything about me and I couldn't imagine she would betray me.

I never should've confided in her and told her what really brought me here and who I really was. Now it seemed that someone knew about my past and was trying to frighten me into running again.

Sadly, I knew I could no longer trust Audrey. I had to figure out what my next move would be, and where I could go until I found out who was following me and why. I couldn't go to the police, and I couldn't go home because my husband might be there and all hell would break loose if he found out what was really going on.

Fate took care of the decision for me, and I'd never make it home.

We had a lot of briefs to go over and chose to meet right after lunch. Once everyone had all the information needed to proceed with this case, and we hoped that we would get an acquittal for the defendant, but in all honesty I was not perfectly sure of his innocence. While I made phone calls to the necessary parties to help with the defense, dealing with other clients first to make sure my calendar was clear to handle this murder trial, Michelle brought me coffee and a muffin and several other papers the group needed to assess before going into court.

Back at work, I was sitting at my desk and going over the transcripts with my legal team. As we started to read some of the transcripts from the depositions taken by my team from the witnesses for the prosecution, and others taken by their team of our major witnesses, I began feeling strange, first hot then cold, and decided to go to the ladies' room and put some cold water on my face.

When I got up to go to the ladies' room, no one expected the loud thud that followed. No one — including Tony, who showed up pretending to bring me some coffee, which I already had — did anything to help me. Pretending to care, Tony waited quite a while before he attempted to do CPR and chest compressions, but he had no idea what he was doing.

I felt like I was watching myself while floating over the body that he was attempting to revive. My past came flooding back to me while I watched and prayed I would remain part of the present. I'd always wanted to be a dancer and become one of the Rockettes. But, fate had something else in store for me.

I saw myself taking dancing lessons on Hunts Point in the Bronx as Nettie and Jeannie Arcaro conducted the lessons. I saw my poor sister, waddling across the floor without any form and not very graceful. I could see myself learning new steps and tapping, while my poor sister was ready for a career as a klutz, and the dear thing could not even stand on toe shoes or walk properly with her ballet slippers. Class began and we all had fun. When it was over my mom took us out for a special treat.

School was not hard for me … I was really smart. I skipped a grade in junior high when I made the SP class, and I learned the hard way that with anything less than a ninety average you were ostracized by the teachers of the class for not being at the right level.

I spent two years in junior high and then I went to high school, where I really didn't want to be. I wanted to go to beauty and modeling school and then become a secretary. Instead I decided to go to college and get my BA. I enjoyed the experience, and decided to take a run at law school, never figuring that I'd become the managing partner in a law firm and have need for my own skills someday.

At the time I graduated high school I was more interested in boys than dealing with term papers and tests. But, my sister encouraged me and told me that I was smart and it would be a waste not to use my intelligence.

I graduated from law school, passed the bar, and then focused on getting married. But, I never told Tony about my past, the mistakes I made, or why I'd gotten divorced in the first place. How could he understand what I had to do in order to make money to take care of my kids and myself without getting caught?

As the chest compressions continued and someone finally called for help, I remembered the red car that had been tailing me on the way to my office, and the face hidden behind the hat and facemask. No matter how hard I'd tried to lose the driver of the car, they'd persisted in following me.

It was starting to come back to me. I felt like I was about to come back to the present when there was a burning sting in my arm. I opened my eyes for a second and saw the strange man who'd been in the office earlier. Tony turned around and smiled at him.

For some reason Audrey was in my office, but I have no idea why she was there. She worked in Staten Island; so why was she here? The cold look in Audrey's eyes frightened me, but she just stood there staring at me before putting on her coat to leave. She turned around when she got to the door and smiled at me. Her smile sent chills down my spine. Was she in it with Tony? Were they lovers or was I imagining things?

I heard the medics say that after five minutes there was no hope for me; my brain cells were dying. *What would the world going to do without me?* I wondered.

The problem was that everyone stood around, frozen, and no one called 911. No one moved. It was like they'd all forgotten what to do in an emergency situation. Even Tony, who'd brought coffee, just shook his head and stood there staring at me, doing nothing. When they finally realized I wasn't moving, someone checked my neck and wrists for a pulse. It was slow and uneven; almost nonexistent.

At that point, apparently Michelle figured it was time to call 911. Tony tried to grab the phone out of her hand, but she finally made the call. Unfortunately, it was too late for me and my brain cells. Feigning that he cared, Tony pretended to do chest compressions until the paramedics came and took over.

In 27 minutes, my life was pulled out from under me like the proverbial run, all because no one did anything, no one believed I was in danger. No one seemed to care. Just 27 minutes and my voice was silenced, forever.

So, why the hell did I just keel over and die? I wasn't sure. It was ruled a massive heart attack, but my jury was still out on that one. Could it have been something else? Maybe someone put a little something in my juice drink after exercise class?

I'd worked all my life and put my heart and soul into everything I ever did. I run the office I worked in better than a well-oiled ship. People could come to me for advice on their personal lives and businesses, and I would make sure that their problems got solved. Working was great, but I overworked myself and now look where I was.

Did I imagine seeing Audrey in my office? Could it have been someone else? Either way, it was not going to change my situation. How was anyone going to know what really happened to me and why when no one thought it was foul play? Now I wouldn't be there to protect my kids.

I knew it was too late and my fate had now been written in stone. I hovered over my body and saw Tony standing there with a smirk on his face. He glanced over his shoulder as his assistant, Rosalina, came barreling through the door. She pretended to comfort him, but not before he whispered in my ear, "Die, Maria! Die! Do everyone a favor and just go!" I fought to speak, but nothing came out of my mouth and I still clung to life with all my might.

At the hospital, dear f-ing Tony wanted them to pull the plug immediately. He called my kids, but didn't call my sister until five hours after I got to the hospital. Once she found out what had happened to me, she called in the head of neurology and demanded to speak with everyone handling my case.

My sister's efforts got me a stay of execution for a month. She came to the hospital every morning, monitored my care, and checked on me every night.

Tony, on the other hand, was just biding his time. He even had his girlfriend/assistant come to the hospital pretending to be my caring friend. Rosalina was a real piece of work. Staring at me and willing me to die, she and Tony looked like they would break out in song and dance if and when I went.

My sister was more than upset. Family members came and went, but no one except my sister realized what Tony really wanted. She knew he was just pretending to care. With him never missing a day of work and asking my sister if she could be there every morning, how could anyone not wonder just how much he cared? Of course, *he didn't!*

Tony had been cheating on me for a long time, and for whatever reason Rosalina seemed to be the one who finally caught his eye and kept it. My sister and my children were the only ones who really cared about me.

As I lay there with the tubes and machines keeping me alive, I wondered why he'd waited so long to call for help for me. What did he have to gain besides his freedom?

Each morning when my sister came to the hospital, Tony made sure to make himself scarce. He called her every morning, telling her he had business meetings, and stuff at work and would come by to see me later in the day.

Every time he entered my room the heart monitors went off; no one realized it is a signal from me to keep him away. I was so glad I was never left alone with this monster. Unfortunately, he had the final say in what happened with my care. He eventually had me moved me into Palliative Care, which was what Dr. Fredricks and others had wanted from day one.

Palliative Care was quiet, and I knew they were about to remove the tubes and machines that were keeping me alive. Tony even convinced the doctor to give me more much more morphine than normal, claiming that I was in pain. How would he know?

"Morphine," I heard the nurse say, "speeds up death." Thanks so much for caring.

My sister tried her best to halt things, calling hospitals all over the world that dealt with traumatic brain injury. Every one of them said that if

I woke up and was off the machines, they would help with my recovery.

They removed all life support, and I just lay there waiting for the inevitable to come. My sister was holding my hand, and my children had come to say their final goodbyes. At 11:30 p.m., I took my final breath.

From the either, I heard Tony talking to someone, whispering so no one would hear. The smile on his face was quite telling, and the cunning look of victory let me know that he was anything but sad about me being gone.

My sister planned my funeral and Tony refused to pay for it. Imagine not wanting to pay for your own wife's funeral and getting angry when you're told it's your responsibility. Then, he showed up with his girlfriend, who was crying crocodile tears. The fake outpouring of grief would've made me lose my lunch, if I were alive. To top it off, my miserable, piece-of-dirt husband didn't even think it was necessary to buy a quality headstone to mark my grave. Thank God, my sister and my children made sure I got one. It was a lovely headstone, too, with a special inscription that reads: *Here lies Maria D. Wonderful mother, sister, friend, aunt, and special person.*

The funeral was on a Friday morning. The day was bleak, but more than three hundred people attended. It seemed like everyone had loved me, except Tony.

The service was somber. My sister read several poems, my law partner spoke, and was followed by my brother. Finally, Tony delivered what I'm sure he thought would come across as a heartfelt speech, but it fell flat.

After the service was over and they were all stuffed into a limo, we left for the cemetery. The ride was quiet, with no one speaking. There was a dark haired woman who remained at Tony's side the entire time.

The rabbi and several others spoke at graveside. When the service was over the family — minus Tony, his "guest," and his two daughters —went to the local diner for lunch.

Now here I am, six feet under, wearing the same outfit every day, with no one to talk to and nowhere to go. Did Tony have an insurance policy on me that paid out big? Is he living high on the hog with money earned by my death? I can't help my family and I can't tell anyone that I think I was murdered. Who will grant me justice?

Detective Florio of the New Jersey Police Department had been my friend for many years, and something about my death bothered him. After reading my file, he decided to do some investigating on his own. He reviewed the doctor's notes, interviewed the ER doctors, and tried to get a handle on my physical condition before my death.

He was stumped when he learned that my test results came back negative and that no one understood why I'd had a massive heart attack. He wondered if someone tampered with my blood pressure medicine or drugged my coffee. *Did someone want her dead?*

One person from the funeral stuck out in Detective Florio's mind — Rosalina. She and Tony were attached at the hip during the whole service. He talked to my sister and she remembered her coming to the hospital to visit me many times, always appearing forlorn and upset. My sister told the detective that was all an act.

Searching for answers in my case would not be easy, but the good detective just might have the right connections to find out the truth.

Time moved on and the case was unresolved, but Detective Florio was still working on it. He wouldn't give up until he found out what really happened to me.

My sister also told the detective what she found when she went to get my clothes and my personal effects. Tony had put everything of mine into 21 plastic trash bags, but most of my more expensive coats, dresses, and bags were missing. When she asked Tony where the rest they were, he claimed that was everything. He wouldn't even allow her into my room to check the closets. She could tell by his answers that he was lying, and that the clothes either wound up with some of his relatives or his girlfriend or he sold them for a profit.

Detective Florio suspected that Tony had a life insurance policy on me that would pay off big time when I was gone. The main problem he was facing was not being able to get a search warrant because he was working on this in his spare time — it wasn't an official investigation.

PART 2
Retribution

I might've been buried and forgotten by Tony, but my sister was still thinking about me every day. Felicity felt like she couldn't let another day go by knowing Tony was out there enjoying life, having and fun without a care in the world. She called Detective Florio and they decided to bring in a private investigator to help find out the dirt on Tony and what he was doing. The detective decided to use Frank, who was the best PI in town and a part of the Fata Law Firm. When he contacted him, he immediately agreed to help.

Frank asked for the files related to my death, got the hospital records, and decided to start with the accounts Tony had given to the EMTs, the ER staff, and the hospital about what he thought happened that day. Not surprisingly, each account was different. No one else had thought to check into this.

First he said I fell over in the office. Then he said he thought I fell over and was pretending to have a heart attack, while winking at him to indicate it was a joke. In reality, I was twitching and in pain.

Next, he began checking the notes in medical records of the doctors who'd taken care of me. He noticed several different suggestions of what was wrong, but no one thought to do a tox screen to check to see if anything was in my bloodstream that shouldn't be there. Another red flag was that no one checked my records with the doctor I'd seen just the day before.

Frank became more suspicious and questioned Tony while he was at work at his pharmacy. Of course, his new main squeeze, Rosalina, stood there holding his hand while he pretended to be upset over my death.

Next, he questioned the ER and ICU staff at the hospital I was in before being placed in Palliative Care. He also interviewed the neurologist, and was not impressed with him or his assessment. He also didn't care for the doctor that finally got me moved into Palliative Care against my sister's wishes.

Somewhere in my file cabinet was a signed health proxy, giving my sister my power of attorney, but no one thought to find it or Tony had found it and torn it up. He'd even tried to find and hide my will, but it was in a safety deposit box I shared with my sister and she was smart enough to keep it from him.

After his final interview, Frank wrote up a report stating that someone wanted me out of the way. He listed several things he found suspicious including the fact that no one asked the doctors to look further into what caused my condition and that my husband was anxious to pull the plug on my life support.

I was afraid that Tony was going to get away with what he had planned all along; living off my life insurance policy, moving in with Rosalina.

As Detective Florio continued to look into my death, he decided to talk to Tony again. When he went to the pharmacy, he found out Tony had sold it to another pharmacist and moved away. No one knew his new address.

Apparently, Tony decided it would be wise to change his appearance and start over again. He even changed professions. He enrolled in the LA beauty school and got his license. He then dyed his hair red with blond streaks, and became Mr. Frank. He had hopes of catering to the Hollywood set.

He opened his own beauty shop in his new location. He had a new identity, new driver's license and new Social Security number. Somehow, he'd managed to pull this off without a hitch.

Would anyone realize who he really was? Just how many women did he have working for him? Would one of them fall prey to his wiles and be the next one silenced in 27 minutes? Knowing Frank as I did, I knew he was not done yet.

I'm still here behind the stones waiting for the truth to triumph over the lies. I hope the truth hasn't been buried with me. Justice will come when he least expects it! I know who that is!

The Betrayal

My name is Dr. Goldman, and I guess my story began over twelve years ago with a simple comprehensive examination of my patient. Cursory exam of her teeth, gums and mouth done, I instructed the nurse to take a full set of x-rays. Leaving Lisa to take the films, I went into my office and returned some phone calls.

Twenty minutes later, the films were developed and showed nothing more than two small cavities that I felt could wait to be filled. But, on the lower left side there was something dark and not very big that looked like she was losing some bone. So, not thinking anything of it and not wanting to alarm the patient, I never told her about it.

I cleaned her teeth, suggested that she might need a root canal on one or two in the future. I told her to come back in three months, which she did. Since the films were taken just three months before, I never bothered to check on that little dark spot, and she never complained of any pain in the lower left quadrant of her mouth. After I filled the two small cavities she left.

When she came back the next week for a cleaning I decided to take films of the area where the cavities were filled, not wanting to deal with the lower left side until the next time she needed a full set of films. For one reason, I thought it was nothing, and the other was I really wanted the insurance company to pay for the films, and they would not cover another set this year.

The patient, whose name I will withhold, never complained about anything, until one Saturday morning she stated that something in the upper left hand quadrant of her mouth was bothering her. I finally did take a film and felt a root canal was in order. This would be big money; since I suggested that she get a gold tooth. The entire procedure from start to finish would be over $3,000, which she would have to pay out of pocket and wait to be compensated by her insurance company. I never liked to wait for *my* money.

Reminding myself about that little dark spot, I made up an excuse that I should recheck the bottom to make sure she had no other teeth that required a root canal or had more cavities. This time the dark spot looked a little bigger, but it was nothing I thought should concern her or me.

The patient came to see me on a regular basis from 2002-2013. Trying to give this patient the best care, I created my own comprehensive program for her: sets of x-rays taken on a regular basis, plus cleanings every three or four months, as well as assessments of gum problems, cavities, and root canals that needed to be done.

Seeing something on the x-ray that looked like a dark shadow, I discounted it as not related to her gums or teeth. Seeing it several more times on each x-ray, I thought the person doing the x-rays might have left a fingerprint, smudge, or maybe moved the film so that the picture came out with a dark spot. I never really gave it much thought, and never mentioned it to the patient.

After a while, I realized the patient needed five root canals, crowns, and about eighteen cavities filled. That dark spot would have to take a back seat for a while. I never really thought, and still don't think, that it was anything to worry about.

Low and behold, in 2013 the patient decided — I have no idea why — to see another dentist, and then the you-know-what really hit the fan. Why did she have to make such a big fuss over nothing? Why didn't she just come back to me to find out what it was, instead of going to another dentist and then to a surgeon to retake the films and then a CAT scan?

What a witch. She's always complaining and never really caring about all the times I got her in without an appointment and wanted to help her. I even gave her a discount on some of the work. But no, she had to sue me and file a malpractice suit against me. How ungrateful!

Mistakes are made sometimes, and full disclosure is not always in the patient's best interest.

So what if I never told her? I handled her cavities, did tons of root canals and the major work that would bring me more billable hours. A stupid cyst and losing three teeth. Big deal! She could get implants or a bridge.

***

The dentist needs to learn his lesson, and it is time for him to pay for what he did. His voice lingers in my mind and my ears every day. I look in the mirror and see that the left side of my face looks sunken in and hollow. I can't feel the left side of my jaw on the bottom, and now I even wear braces. I've been though all of this and he's walking around scot-free; showing no remorse. There are other patients, I'm sure, who will pay for his negligence just like I did. It's time to explain what happens when a doctor does not care, is negligent, and pretends to want to help you but in reality only wants to fill his pockets with money.

***

Dr. Goldman arrived early one morning and was greeted by two men in dark suits. Dr. Goldman questioned them and asked if they were new patients. They said yes. But, when entering the office Dr. Goldman became the patient, and the end result would be much worse for him than what happened to the person with a cyst who lost three teeth. His proscribed treatment: no Novocain, no lidocaine, just pliers for his extractions. To keep him quiet during this procedure, they administered a drug that would make him unable to speak or move.

Changing into what appeared to be EMT uniforms, the men carried the doctor out of his office. No one witnessed him leaving; the doctor had arrived an hour before office hours to complete some paperwork and had been the only one in the building besides the two men he found in his office.

Leaving the building, the men loaded Dr. Goldman into an ambulance, which was parked right outside the office. Dr. Goldman was taken to a special place where his body was drained of all fluids. It was then placed in a special casket with a wooden tooth carved on top of it, which rests in a grave under an unmarked stone.

The Imposters

In the passenger seat of each limo was a person. Each yielded some type of hold or power over so many individuals, pretending to be someone they were not.

The first — let's call him The Musician — was a man claiming to have written many concertos, sonatas, and even a waltz he claimed was stolen by one of the greatest composers ever. He claimed he was reborn and is over 200 years old. Delusional to say the least, yet many believed his story. Never committing to playing in front of anyone or regaling audiences with his talent, he managed to create CD's, albums, and even placed what he claimed were his compositions on iTunes for all to hear.

But this man was tone deaf, could not read music, and his only talent was fraud. The radio in the limo blared music from a rock station, and he pretended to sing along with the rap singer.

The limo entered the dark, wooded area, desolate and dank and filled with an acrid smell that, had his windows been opened, would have caused nausea to overcome him or anyone close by.

As this man was the first of five to enter this area, you, the reader, might be wondering why. All five had sinned and would pay for their crimes. All had used their ill-gotten gains to benefit their wants, whether it be expensive cars, homes, or even the best of imported wines. All had made that one big mistake by lying to one powerful, whose tolerance or for being conned, duped, or lied to on a scale of one to ten was below freezing.

As The Musician's limo approached the main gate, someone came out and the limo stopped. Opening his door, he found himself facing a man he'd hoped never to see again. Trying to think of what to say and a way out of what was about to happen, he faltered with his speech, hoping that he could convince this man he might be mistaken; but he couldn't.

"You will come with me. Do not speak, do not say anything; just walk."

With four men flanking him on all sides and one carrying a gun, holding it directly at the back of his head, he had no choice but to comply.

He was the first to be lowered into his unmarked coffin. Not the best for any of these people, just a pine box with either an X or a Y to determine male or female.

***

The second car carried a would be actress who used her talents to not only fleece her fellow actors, but to create her own escort business for highly influential men and women, using what she'd taped and learned about them to blackmail them into paying her a huge fee just to stay quiet. Senators, congressmen, and women were among her clients, and this person had no qualms about charging over the top fees for the services being rendered. Each one hoped to benefit from the services, and each one learned the hard way that she should not have been trusted. Not making it on the silver screen because her acting skills were way below par—but at one time she was quite beautiful and could entice men into her lair— this would be star hoped to win the award, or academy of her life, when pleading for mercy. She came in last.

Next in line was a teenage boy who was into drugs, alcohol, extortion, and gambling. Working for a man high up in a powerful organization, he used his connections to take advantage of his unsuspecting clients, friends, and family. Selling drugs to his friends at an inflated rate in order to profit was one thing he did. But, selling bad drugs or drugs that could injure someone quite badly was only part of his crime. Like the actress and the dentist, he showed no remorse for his actions, and could not understand why he was chosen to be placed beneath a stone.

The fourth person was a scientist whose life's work was to find a cure for Alzheimer's, but instead found a drug that would speed up the course of the disease while making the caregivers think that their loved ones might be cured.

The limo came to a stop next to a distinguished looking man in a black suit, who was standing with his hand held out, holding several pills and a glass of ice water. The fourth man started to back away, but someone else pushed him ahead and stopped him in his tracks, then held him in place. The man with the pills dropped them into the water, where they dissolved, and then handed it to the man to drink. He knew he had no choice in the matter, and while he did not want to feel the effects of whatever was in that glass, he had no choice but to drink it. The end did not come quickly, and the results were startling. The fourth man began ranting, raving, and seeing things, and then admitted what he had done, but showed not an ounce of remorse.

The final limo carried an older woman with thin gray hair and wearing a gray shirt and pants. She was a prison warden in her younger years, and had prided herself on abusing the prisoners just for the sport of it. As the limo was about to come to a halt she reflected about all that she had done to so many, and as she remembered what she had done to one young woman she smiled.

Beatings, drugs given, solitary, and withholding meds and meals were just a few of her tactics. The young and beautiful girl began to wither away all because someone had wrongly accused her of murder and no one believed in her innocence. This prison was maximum security.

The woman in the limo learned what her fate was going to be as the car stopped and she found herself facing the families of many she had wronged. Within the cemetery this woman faced the parents of the young girl, who took her own life, the father of another who lived out her years in a sanitarium, and one more whose violent end was so horrific that it still haunted her family each time they remembered how they'd found her.

All five limos had stopped, and all of those that were finding out what their fates would be were given one chance to repent; to reflect and ask for forgiveness before sentence was passed and executed. First was the musician, whose life was spent stealing the music and songs of others and claiming them for his own. The second was the actress, the third the young teen on drugs, the fourth the scientist, and fifth the warden, each one about to face their maker.

The first coffin was lowered, and the fate of the musician was sealed. The rest had a chance, but would they take it or would they decide that death was the answer to set them free?

The actress feigned being upset and claimed she wanted another chance. The teenage boy stared straight ahead and said nothing, but had an odd grin on his face as if he thought someone might save him at the last minute. The next was the scientist, who was beginning to feel the effects of the drugs he had been forced to take and no longer had any sense of reality. The last and most vicious, the warden, seemed cold, austere, and unmoved.

What do you think their fate should be? Would you lower the coffins and place them behind the unmarked stones? Would you forgive their sins? You decide!

The Competitor

Co-Authored with Jake Swerdloff

There are many lessons to be learned from what happens to a popular baseball legend who had it all … money, fame, and a prime position on a major league baseball team, where he was captain of the team and had women dropping at his feet.

Brian Thompson was a star catcher on a major league baseball team. Playing for a while in the minors, he was a first draft pick. Scouts on at least ten teams hoped he'd play for their team, but choosing the one in his hometown just seemed like the right fit. Never worrying about being tossed aside, he scored in every game, and tagged players from the opposing team out before they could reach home plate. Brian was a star player, and his teammates respected his skills, loyalty to the team, and his friendship.

But beneath his handsome face lurked an evil, jealous, and heartless young man that would often torture his younger brother, make him do his chores, take his mother for granted, and be rude to adults in public. Yet on the field he was like another person. Brian is under the next stone shaped like a baseball glove. Brian will explain in his own voice and words why he is now a Face Behind that magnificent Marble Stone.

***

I lived and breathed baseball. As the team's number one batter and catcher, I never thought that this day would come, but it did. After everything I had done for that team and the manager, how could they stab me in the back and say that I belonged in the minors when my batting average had always been high? So what if I had a brief slump. Everyone did at times. My batting average is between 287 and 300 … what more could you ask of someone still young enough to play the game at age thirty? I never missed a practice, and was always there to help a new teammate. So, why did they need this new guy, José, to come in straight from high school? He was a real punk … who at just eighteen years old was drafted for the purpose of taking my place.

It started about six months ago when I got called into the manager's office and he read me the riot act. "Brian, you've been playing for this team for over eight years, and your batting average and skills have always been first rate. Obviously the last year has been rough. Divorcing your wife, taking steroids, and not focusing on the game are definite signs that a change needs to be made, and that it's more than just a slump.

José is young and has skills, and we're bringing him here from Puerto Rico after graduating high school. He's smart, his average is okay, and he's getting a full ride on this team. With you being captain of the team again this year, I am counting on you to show him the ropes, introduce him to the team, and hopefully understand that now he's taking your position as catcher.

Figuring out another spot for you will take time. Coach Jenkins feels that you should sit out for a while until he finds another spot for you on the team. Coach Jennings disagrees and feels that Jose should start out in left field and see where it goes from there, and hopefully our investment in him will be worth it."

Listening to him, all I wanted to do was take a bat and beat him over the head, but I restrained myself. Clenching my fists behind my back, holding back my scowl and praying that I could withstand what was coming my way, I had to figure out a plan to get rid of this new guy before he got too comfortable.

Adam Thompson was the assistant captain and pitcher on this team. Somehow, I had to make sure he was on my side without drawing too much attention to the fact that I hated this kid already and wanted him off the team.

Carlos Morales might be difficult to bring to my side, as he and José were both Latinos. Mark Ross and Tim Edwards played outfield and were just okay players, but the team was close to coming in first and being in the playoffs, and we have only a few more weeks to get there. If we won all, or at least most of the remaining games, we had a good shot at being in the playoffs, and I intended to play catcher, not this green guy.

Coming back to the present, I heard the coach ask me if I understood his position, and I decide to not respond. Let him wonder what I was thinking and let him stew a while, because a plan was being formulated as he spoke, and my goal was to make sure that José Rivera was past tense really soon … in more ways than one.

José was scheduled to arrive on Monday of the following week, which gave me enough time to formulate my plan, pretend to want to help him, and hopefully regain my position even before he showed up. Having been promised a lucrative career and a great contract, this kid would make more money than most people his age would ever see in a lifetime.

Why did he have to take my spot? What about him was better than me? Supposedly his batting average was 330, and that was on the low side for him. At times he batted at an average of 335 and more. He was unstoppable, and hit at least two homeruns every game, was never called out, and never dropped a ball. Mr. Perfect, or so they said. But, what I had in store for him … well, you just wait and see! No one screwed around with me.

Biding my time would be the answer, because if I came on too strong and acted the way I really felt, it might alert everyone that I was up to something. So, I asked him to go out for a couple of brews with the team after the first game, pretending to be his close bud and glad that he was adding some real strength to the team. After all, we were basically in a slump, and I felt that with the two of us we might just pull off a win for the series this year. But, first I had to make sure that my position was safe and that he might have some serious slips, but nothing too obvious.

The local hangout, Frankie's on the Waterfront, was the team's bar of choice. Getting José to join us was the first step in my plan. Going to the local supermarket, I picked up what I needed in order to implement step two. Slow and easy I would make sure that I tainted his drinks, but not all at once. Arsenic was my poison of choice, and getting some of it from rat poison was not difficult at all. Making sure it wound up in his drink needed planning.

Talking with José, I learned that he was taking allergy medicine for his serious hay fever, and the medication would not mix well with alcohol. Therefore, that meant using the poison would not be the way to go, so I thought of a better idea.

My mom was on Coumadin and took lisinopril for her high blood pressure, along with dilitiazem. I thought that using a low dose of Coumadin might work. The allergy pills were white and 10 mg of Coumadin in pill form was white too, so he wouldn't notice the switch.

Coach Jenkins called practice that night at seven to go over the new lineup, positions, and the goal for the team. Hoping that the newest player would bring us some wins, he blatantly told me he would be the new catcher and I would now play in the outfield. Trying to assert myself and ask why, he refused to allow me to finish my thought, and said if I wanted to remain with the team I needed to be a team player, and that we needed Jose to help us win some games. "You keep dropping the ball, you never get anyone out at home plate, and your batting average is way below 300 now. You're lucky we don't sack you."

I could feel my temper rising, so I just walked away and said nothing. Now I would have to escalate my plan and make sure that José's stay with the team would be short lived. When and how would I do it? Could I confide in anyone? Was anyone else in the same boat as me? Who else's position was being challenged, and who could I trust?

As I looked around the team I realized that my good friend Mario had just come from a team in Texas to ours in New Orleans, and he, too, was hoping to be a star, as a pitcher. But, Felix was solid in the position for now, although the coach said Mario just might get a chance if Felix lost the first game.

Our team consisted of Adam Thompson, Carlos Morales, Tim Edwards, Zach Hughes, Manny Salazar, Mike Palmer, Daniel Peters, Ned Smith, and Jorge Ramsey. In addition, the bench was filled with at least two dozen more players sitting there hoping to be put in the game, and the bullpen housed pitchers waiting in case the starting pitcher ran into trouble.

These guys were great, but the coach said that no one was safe, and now that Felix had been sent to us from a team in Chicago, and José from a high school baseball team in Puerto Rico, some of us really felt the heat … and not from the sun.

Planning was what was needed, but I had to be careful not to tip my hand. Outfield was not my favorite position, but pretending and acting like it did not matter and taking the change in stride was the first step in making sure that no one would suspect me when the final curtain fell on Jose.

Jose was a nice guy but cocky in some respects. Imagine getting picked for the majors right out of high school at nineteen years of age. His father was the coach of his team and had invited some of the major league coaches to watch the games since he had played for a major league team at one time. Naturally, not everyone on the team was thrilled with the kid, and him taking my place as catcher put him on my list as someone who needed to be taught more than just a lesson.

The playoffs would take place from September 1 until October 6, according to the league and our coach. Practice would be mandatory. Losses would not be tolerated, and any major player like pitchers, catchers, or anyone manning a base would be cut, changed, or even sacked if not holding their own. Batting averages had better be above average, and no matter what position you played you had better get a run.

How was I to rid the team of him and protect myself and my position? As the day progressed my plan came into mind and I had to make sure that what I was going to do to Jose would not come back at me. How dare he come here and just take over my position? Getting to know him better, I found out that he had a medical problem that required that he take blood thinners, and he should not be drinking at all. This clicked in my mind, so I Googled blood thinners and came up with several that just might serve my purpose and not be detected right away. I realized that it might not be so difficult at all.

His first game was today and I had to play outfield and he, of course, catcher. The game went okay and the coach was thrilled that we finally took one, but not by much. José did okay but missed some catches, and although they were considered foul balls he still could have cost us the game. So, I decided to be a pal and tell him he'd had a great first game, and offered to take him for pizza with the other guys to show that we were on the same team; but, of course, not on the same page.

Talking with him more, he loosened up about his medical problem and the plan formulated in my mind. My mom took Coumadin, so why not put some in one of his drinks? It would go unnoticed. Ten milligrams was about the right dose … my mom took two fives, and had so many bottles of it she wouldn't even know that some were missing.

The following day at practice he asked if I could get him some water, but that would not be the drink of choice to place a white ground up pill in, so I suggested some ginger ale or Coke. He agreed to the ginger ale, and I opened the bottle, put in the ground powder, and closed it, hoping he would not realize that it had already been opened. But if he did I would just say I opened it for him, knowing he would be quite thirsty. Drinking it down, he appeared fine. But the dose I was giving him might not cause the bleed out right away.

Practice went okay, but José felt kind of tired and his face was getting pale. Offering to get him another soda, I added a stronger dose of the ground up medication this time, hoping that it might do the trick. Changing my mind, I poured it out.

For some reason I had a change of heart, and realized that it was not his fault. What was happening to me was the fault of the coaches for thinking I was not fit. But José fainted and was taken to the hospital, where they discovered a bleed out in his left shoulder. The outcome of the surgery was still up in the air.

Competition brings out the worst in people, and it had done the same to me. Someone realized what I had done when I went to get the second ginger ale. I didn't know how this person saw what I did, but I denied it when I was questioned by the coaches and the hospital staff. "Where would I get whatever you think I put in his drink? I just gave him a soda because he was thirsty, and you claim I spiked it with something?"

Someone else wanted José gone, not just me. What they found in the Coke he drank, which I did not give him, was five milligrams of morphine. Someone had chopped up some codeine pills and added them as well. That's why he is now under the next stone, six feet under. But someone wanted me to join him and did the same thing to me.

My name is Brian and competition can be deadly. So much for remorse. I only hope the person who did this to me and José gets what he deserves.

Journey to Nowhere

All I had with me was my suitcase and the clothes on my back. I looked straight ahead of me and saw an endless dirt road, which extended for miles and miles. Wearing my lucky old beat up hat and my woolen coat, I left home early that morning to decide my fate.

My day began with breakfast, going to work at the bank, and coming home to an all but empty apartment with just my faithful dog for company. I felt as though I was going through the motions of life, and my life resembled an old movie or rerun of a television program every day. Life had become mundane, with no challenges ahead and nothing to look forward to. I got up at the same time every day, went to work, and came home.

I was president of the largest bank in this town. It was not a very exciting job, but the money was good and it paid for my kids' school tuition fees and their various extra-curricular activities. There was even money for my soon to be ex-wife to shop wherever and whenever she wanted.

My wife, who never had to work a day in her life, said she was bored and I provided her with no excitement. She had been going to the gym and working out, and had met someone else there. After knowing him for just one month, she'd decided to take herself and my children to live with this total stranger. She even managed to get herself a job as a copy editor at the local newspaper in the area where she was moving. The man she'd met was the paper's editor, and I could not see how his job was any more exciting than mine was. However, he was ten years younger than me, and that seemed to be the draw.

Watching them leave and feeling a tangled mixture of emotions, I realized that I could not make a difference in other people's lives. I needed to start with my own. But staring into her new paramour's face as he got into his car with my family,

I had an uneasy feeling. His eyes stared straight at me and his smile was cold and frightening. He looked evil. He did not speak directly to me and my kids were shaking with fear. My wife told me it would be better this way, and she got into the car and never looked back.

I stood there staring at the back of the car until it disappeared. I could not believe what had happened, nor would I ever believe that I had no choice but to let it. My children were my life, and I could not think about living the rest of it without them However, Jana felt that since I bored her to death with my day at the bank, and nothing much ever happened to excite her during her days, this young guy, whose face looked cold and demonic, was the right one for her. It was as if he had her under a spell.

I began to think of places that I could go and where I could spend the rest of my life. I couldn't even think that far ahead. I wandered down the road until I came to a small body of water that was surrounded by trees and grass. There was no one in sight. It was pitch black. The sky was covered with clouds so dark and ominous that I stood frozen to the spot and couldn't move. The air was damp and yet I felt nothing. I was neither hot nor cold. I felt numb. Feeling nothing but pain in my heart and fear that someone would finally find me and make me go back to the life I had before, I knew that I had to make a move in some direction.

I began contemplating my next step. I didn't know where I was or where the road would lead me. It was so dark that I decided to stay where I was until morning. However, that decision was not so easy to fulfill. I saw a light coming towards me from a distance. I hid behind a tree, or at least I tried to, but I was wearing a yellow shirt and the driver must have seen me from a distance. He got out and walked in my direction. Being in an isolated area, I didn't know where to go or where to run. I just stood there like a statue, hoping that I would look like part of the scenery. As he came closer, I realized that he was a police officer and might recognize me and take me back home.

He drew closer, but before he could approach close enough to speak I heard the crackling of his radio and he stopped in his tracks, but not before looking me straight in the eye with his cold eyes and icy stare. His smile sent chills down my spine, and I prayed he would not come any closer.

Suddenly, he turned and returned to his car, and I breathed a huge sigh of relief. I had thought for a minute that he was the same man who had taken my family away from me. However, from a distance I could not be sure. I passed the night in that place, rooted to the spot, afraid and unsure of myself. With the coming of daylight I summoned what remained of my courage and made my way home. That very day, things began to change.

***

My head began to hurt and I couldn't see where I was going. I had just been to the eye doctor, and he had given me a new prescription for distance glasses. He assured me that wearing them would make things look much clearer, that the glasses would help me not only see where I was, but also where I needed to go. That remark seemed strange at the time, but I just thought he was trying to make me feel better. Little did I know that things would change radically for me and I would have no idea how or why.

Putting on the new glasses, I began walking, with no idea where I might end up. I came to what I thought was a small town. I must have been walking for over an hour before coming to this place. Everything in the town was new and in pristine condition. All of the people were older and looked like they were going about their business without noticing or stopping to speak with anyone who came their way. Everyone was dressed alike, everyone looked alike, and yet no one said a word. All of the stores were well kept but had no customers in them. All of them had one person standing at a cash register waiting to check out an order, but no one entered any of the stores.

I began adjusting my glasses to make sure that I was seeing clearly when someone tapped me on the shoulder.

"Why aren't you in your proper place, and why are you just wandering around doing nothing? Don't you know that's not the way we do things here? Haven't you been here long enough?"

The man didn't introduce himself or stop to hear my response. He just kept going, saying the same thing. "There is no hope for our young people today. So irresponsible, so undependable and so worthless."

I walked a little further, stopped, and stared at myself in a store window. Staring back at me was a younger man dressed like all of the other people in this town, but it was I, looking at least ten years younger. It seemed that the man knew who I was, or at least he was pretending to know me, but he never called me by name nor told me where I was, or what he thought I was supposed to be doing.

The entire town was about ten blocks long and about five blocks wide. Each block had three or four stores and three or four small houses. Behind each of the stores were wooded areas, and behind that was what looked like gated communities. No one seemed to notice or care that I was there … except for one person.

As I came to the end of the town, I could not believe what I saw. A sign read:

You Are Leaving the Town of

Mundane and No Excitement

Today's Date is January 25, 2025

What had happened to me in between? When I left home, it was 2010. Where had fifteen years gone, and where was I during those years?

Walking out of this town, I came to a fork in the road. There were four signs … the first one read:

**The Road to the Town of Nowhere
Keep Wandering**

The second read:

The Road to the Town of Decisions

The third announced itself as:

The Road to the Town of Surprises

Finally, the fourth read:

**Just Walk in This Direction
and You Will Find Out**

I had no idea what these signs really meant, and since I was really nowhere that I knew, I thought about taking off my glasses and hoping to find myself back where I'd started and in my own home town. However, when I did, nothing changed. I started walking in the direction of the second town, hoping that this town of decisions would help me make some for myself. However, when I got there I knew things were only going to get worse.

Facing me at the entrance of the town was the man who'd taken my family. Facing me with his cold stare and chalky face, he stood there all alone and smiled.

"Where are my kids and Jana?" I asked.

He just stared at me as if I was invisible, and then vanished into thin air. I looked around and saw nothing. I looked straight ahead of me where he'd been standing and I saw something so frightening that I thought I might be hallucinating. Looking straight ahead, I beheld a vision. I could see what looked like a floating ball, and inside the ball, I could see my family.

However, they were no longer my family, they were now his. Each one had been transformed into a carbon copy of this demonic creature. Each sat on a chair or bed, staring into space with a strange grin on his/her face. Just blank stares. Then the vision disappeared. They were under some kind of spell or drugged.

Frightened to think or even move, I just stood where I was and I took off my glasses. I began looking around and saw that I was no longer in the town but on the same road I was walking on when I left home.

I sat down in the middle of road and started to cry. What was happening, and why? All of a sudden, I heard voices and loud yells and screams.

"Happy New Year! It's 2200, and what a great world it is. Welcome to the next century."

Where had the time gone? I'd just been in the year 2025. It seemed that every time I left a place I was sent even further into the future.

I might be on the same road that I'd started my journey on, but my surroundings were different. Instead of the beautiful houses and trees in the once countrified community that I had lived in, the area was totally devoid of any trees or vegetation. The road was no longer paved. It was constructed from hard stones and pebbles. The surrounding area featured burnt out barns and houses that were in total disrepair. I walked along this road hoping to find a small town or any sign of people. What I did find was so frightening I stood there and froze.

In front of me was a community of small children who looked like they were all alone, with no adults in sight. They seemed to be part of some colony. The oldest of these children looked to be about sixteen years old. The rest of the children were lined up in front of me, and one other person that looked about eighteen years of age seemed to be in charge. The date was January 25, 2200.

"Everyone here has a job to do. You will follow our orders. If you disobey, you will be severely punished. None of your parents survived the fire and the attack on this village. You have no other place to go. Everyone here must band together and try to make this place our home.

You will have chores to do and some studies that we decide you must learn. You will also cook and clean for yourselves. Hunting and gathering food is your job if you want to eat and stay alive. There are no more supermarkets, restaurants, or even convenience stores. We do have a small general store where our small community can get certain things that we need. However, there are many animals that you can kill and hunt down and eat. We are lucky to have several cows that can be milked and some hens that might lay some eggs.

You are here and that is all there is to it. Everyone must get to work to build a shelter to live in, or use whatever houses are here. You can rebuild something or just start from scratch. I do not care. Just remember, we are a community and we must stick together and protect ourselves from any strangers from any other villages or cities that might try and come here and take what little we have."

Just as he was about to turn back and go into his house or what appeared as a small house, he saw me standing there looking straight into his cold eyes. I could not believe it. The face that was staring straight at me was a younger version of the man who'd taken my family away so many years ago. This person must be his son or grandson. I froze where I was standing. However, he said nothing. Maybe they couldn't see me clearly, but I could see them.

How could the future of the world turn into what looked like the past? As I was propelled into the future, it felt like the world was moving backwards in time.

As I stood watching the scene before me, someone came up from behind, hit me on the head with something hard, and knocked me out cold.

When I finally woke up, I had a throbbing headache, felt nauseous, and could barely sit up. The left side of my face and head were covered in dried blood. Whatever I was knocked out with had had a sharp edge and really did some major damage to my head and my face.

I could not stand up without feeling dizzy and light-headed. I did not see anyone around. My eyes were having trouble focusing on where I was and my vision was blurry. What had happened to the village and the community where I saw the strange man?

When my vision finally cleared and the throbbing in my head seemed to be subsiding, I took a long look at my surroundings. I was no longer in the same place I was before I was knocked out. I was in an open field with nothing but grass and farmland in the distance. I could not see any barns, farmhouses, or anything. There was no one in sight as far as I could see.

When I was finally able to stand up I knew I needed to decide which way to go. Where should I walk and in what direction? However, all I saw on all four sides were empty fields of green for miles around.

Then out of nowhere, I saw an object coming at me at a high speed from a distance. I tried to get out of its way but I had no idea what it was or who was controlling it. In a flash and a blur someone grabbed my arms and my legs, I was thrown into a vehicle, and something was placed over my head. I could not see anything at all. I tried to scream but nothing came out of my mouth. My screams fell on deaf ears.

After what seemed an age the vehicle stopped, and when I was finally taken out of the vehicle and my eyes uncovered, I was no longer in the village with the children, nor was I in the town of Boredom and Mundane. This was somewhere else. There were people standing on moving sidewalks and cars of sorts that were going at warp speeds high in the air and flying over other layers of traffic.

There were people on phones who were able to not only talk to the person, but see them as well. The stores and the shops clerks and managers did not look human. They looked like droids of some kind. The people had odd stares and their faces seemed fixed with one expression. No one noticed me or seemed to realize that I was different.

Hanging in midair was a calendar that said today's date was January 25, 3000. It would be warm and sunny today, just like yesterday and tomorrow. The temperature would be 75 degrees today, just like yesterday and tomorrow. The name of this town was Stand Still.

I began to rethink what had happened to me so far, and realized that in every place I was and had been, the date was the same, but the year changed each time.

Just as I was about to try and leave this town, I saw the demonic face and cold stare of a young man who seemed frozen in time standing right in front of me. He had not aged at all. His appearance was the same as it was when he came and took my family away from me. Behind him were my wife, Jana, and my children, all looking straight at me with that same cold stare and drugged smile.

As I stood there, uncomprehending and afraid, a voice from somewhere in my dim memory spoke softly from the deepest recesses of my mind, "Welcome to your life. The places might change, but the date will stay the same, and the *glasses* will determine what happens to you. You see, I am the Eye Doctor! Do you see things clearly now?

Crime Pays Off:
Just Don't Get Caught

The year was 2020. I was sitting on a couch in a plain room with nothing but four blank walls staring me in the face. Things were different now. Buildings had no windows, fresh air was pumped in through vents, cars were battery operated, and the outside world did not exist for anyone.

My name is Harold. I was the founder of an Internet company:

www.JustAskHaroldAndHe'llTellYou.com.

Harold … that is, I … was the sole founder and owner of this company. People from everywhere in the world would email me, text me, and call for advice just about every day. I controlled the markets and told stockbrokers which stocks were hot and which were cold. I gave advice to rich executives who needed to make investments in order to liquidate funds and get some quick cash.

My clients made millions and so did I. For a monthly fee and a large commission paid to me, these rich executives were able to make their investments and no one knew where or how they were made. Hidden bank accounts were untraceable and everyone was happy — especially me.

At the risk of sounding egotistical, I have to say that at fifty years of age I was still a genius. I understood the market, and played the horses, slots, or any game of chance. I could tell you how to beat the odds at a roulette table, or teach you how to count cards in Black Jack. Therefore, why was I sitting in a room with four walls, locked away, never to see the outside world again? Because somehow, someway, I was caught. I have only one chance for escape…

Sitting there contemplating my fate, I began to see flashes of things to come … or were they?

I was looking at the wall and saw a man who looked just like me, but it was not me. He had a wife and family, and looked fairly well off. Then, the vision disappeared.

I began thinking of what I should do next. There were no windows, no doors, and the only contact I had with people was through a small vent in the ceiling. Prisons were now escape proof, and once someone was locked away there was no way out. All of my belongings were taken from me when I was placed in this room. But it was not my final stop, or where I would serve out my sorry and miserable life sentence. It was called the Limbo Room, where someone stayed until they figured out what would happen next … or they did it for you.

Sitting at the small desk in the room, I began to see some more of the vision from before. I saw this man at work, and I wanted to learn more about his life and what he did.

He was sitting behind a large desk in an office with plush carpeting and huge bay windows, with a cappuccino machine and a gorgeous young secretary. Wearing a black suit, steel grey shirt, and tie, he looked polished and ready for whatever he was supposed to be doing. Then, the vision disappeared again and I saw the blank wall in front of me.

I was a mogul of industry. Presidents of countries would use my website to help them make major oil deals, and to find out where to get weapons for their armies to fight other countries. I was paid handsomely, and never discussed my clients with anyone. I worked alone except for a small staff that watched the markets in every country, checked oil prices around the world, and dealt with those in charge of selling weapons that were needed by my major clients.

None of these people ever left their offices to go home. Everyone lived in the building where my company was, and everyone was carefully investigated and had to sign some special forms swearing never to divulge what they did to anyone before being hired. No friends or family on the outside were told what they did, and they couldn't have any contact with these people for as long as they worked for me.

So, how was I caught? What was my downfall?

Why did I think my life was so great? It wasn't now, and they'll be coming for me soon. I wasn't going to remain in Limbo much longer. My only hope was to figure out who this man was and what he had to do with my future.

Time moved slowly in Limbo. I was sitting facing the back wall, and this time the vision was clearer. I could hear voices and what people were saying. This man's name was also Harold, and he had a wife, two children, and a girlfriend. Not only was he the president of the bank, but he controlled what investments the money in the bank was used for and where the profits went.

I heard him on the phone with the CFO and CEO of the bank, discussing a possible takeover of another bank. He began to get worried and did not seem to like what he was hearing. Like me, Harold was obviously a man who liked things the way they were, and did not like these two men interfering with the bank's daily operations. Nor does he want the bank takeover.

The vision disappeared again, but now I had some idea of where I might fit in and how I might not be in Limbo forever. However, first I needed to learn more about this man, such as who he was, where he lived, and how his life would make mine better.

Staring at the wall, I hoped to see something, but did not. I heard a voice from the vent saying, "Harold, you have twenty-four hours to go, and then your fate will be decided. Do you understand?" I did not bother to answer. It did not require a response. They could read my mind, and if they did, they would not like what they heard. However, give up I would not, and focus and concentrate I would.

I was never satisfied with my life, and was never happy until I created the internet company. Even then, I was still dissatisfied with my life. I was not very handsome and never really got noticed when I walked down the street, I decided to make myself more marketable and more noticeable by starting this company and helping people get rich.

Starting the company and creating the website was easy. Advertising on YouTube, Facebook, and other sites helped to get the word out that I was there to help anyone that had money to invest and needed to do it quickly and quietly, without the knowledge of the IRS or anyone else in government.

I was getting tired but could not sleep. My survival depended on figuring out who this man was and why he was important to me. The vision was clearer now. I saw him at home with his wife and family. He had dinner, went into his study, and made several calls.

"I need you to take five million dollars and invest it for me in Company A," he said into the phone. "I then need you to take five million more and invest it in Company B. When you're done and the money is where I want it and the investments are made, I want you to sell both of them off. No, do not use company money … use the money in the client funds, and make sure you tell no one.

"My wife wants a new car, my girls want to go on several trips, and I want to make it happen. Do whatever you have to do to get those investments made, and make sure when the stocks go up you sell them electronically and transfer the money into my special account.

"The clients? … Well, they'll be none the wiser. Don't record any of this in their portfolios and do *not* discuss this with anyone. Remember, you owe me and I can destroy you with one phone call."

The man in the room and what he was doing were no different from what I'd done, but he hadn't been caught. He was using cliens' money to fund his own investments.

His wife had inherited a lot of money from an aunt that died, and he had embezzled all of it for his own purposes. She had no idea. As long as he kept her happy and gave her whatever she wanted, she would never question what he was doing with her money or where it was going.

As he sat there waiting for the phone call, his cell phone rang. It was his secretary and girlfriend, who he wanted to dump. She was becoming too demanding and wanted a permanent position in his life. He had it too good to let that happen. He wasn't going to make any changes just yet.

The vision disappeared and the voice coming from the vent said, "You have five more hours and then it is over."

I felt my body shake and hoped that the vision would appear one more time so that I would know the final outcome, and what I had to do in order to get out of Limbo.

Staring straight at the wall, I began to feel a little strange. My arms started to tingle and I felt faint. Since there was just a small cot for me to rest on, I had no choice but to lie down on the hard metal floor. I started to shiver and shake all over, and it wouldn't stop.

What had they put in my lunch? Or was there something in the air coming out of the vent? Was this the end, or was it something else? Maybe I wasn't going to escape my fate. Maybe this was where I would spend eternity for what I had done.

After a few minutes the shaking stopped and I felt better. I heard the voice say, "Four more hours and then…." Looking straight at the wall, I could hear the man speaking.

The voice coming out of the vent in my cell said, "Listen carefully Harold. You'll only hear this once and see it in a flash. Remember all the details or you'll lose and go somewhere much worse than Limbo. Heed my warning."

I looked at the man in the vision and studied his mannerisms and what he was doing. I heard him say the same things to people that I had said before being caught. "Don't worry, that new shipment of cars with the hybrid engines was already sent with the extra packages in the trunks." "Don't worry, the stocks you wanted were purchased and will be worth twice as much in the morning." "Don't worry, Mr. President, no one will know." "Don't worry, Mr. Ambassador, I'll never tell."

Then all of a sudden I realized something. All of my life I was smart. All of my life I did the right thing and towed the mark. I helped all of these people get rich. I helped them using every trick I knew and every get-rich-quick method I knew. So, why was I in Limbo? I was just an ordinary man. I never complained about my life, dull as it was.

Even though I made others rich, and myself too, it had become routine and boring after a while. I must've given someone a wrong tip, or the wrong person got a good stock tip...

The final vision came into view. It was now or never to find out what I must do. Sitting there staring straight at the man, I heard and saw him quite clearly. He was sitting behind his huge oak desk and dictating a letter to someone. When his cell phone rang, we both listened to the person on the phone, and we both heard the same thing. The man's face turned white. He dropped the phone on the floor and just stared at the door in front of him.

The person on the phone had said the other Harold would pay for what he'd done. He said the tip Harold had given him cost the caller everything and more. This was Harold's end.

Time seemed to race ahead, and the next thing I knew the voice coming from the vent said, "You've been here ten years; it is now 2030. Your time in Limbo is up. Did you figure it out yet? You've had all this time to learn what you need to do to get out. Will you look ahead and see your fate or remain?"

The man in the vision was in a room just like mine, but was chained to a chair. Three people were in the room interrogating him. "I swear, I never smuggled drugs or sold rare gems to foreign leaders. I never embezzled money from my clients or stole from their portfolios. I never gave bad stock tips. I invested in the same companies they did. I even gave them shares in my company.

I watched how he did it all those years. I kept a close eye on everything he did. I'm even using his website:

www.JustAskHaroldAndHe'llTellYou.com.

I didn't change anything.

I even had my surgeon make me look like him. I hated him all my life, and I still hate him. I was the one everyone thought would amount to nothing. I was the one who followed the rules and never got in trouble. How could this happen? I'm just a fifty year old investment counselor who got caught up in the frenzy."

Listening to him speak, I realized what I had to do and I hoped it would work. Staring straight at the wall and watching what looked like a live video feed from an interrogation room, I saw the three men turn the man to face the wall. He was instructed to walk toward it and not stop when he came face to face with it. As he walked toward the wall, I walked toward the wall facing me.

The next thing I knew, I was sitting in his house in his chair, with his wife and family. He was now where I used to be — in Limbo or worse. I was now him and he was now me. This time, I vowed to do things to help those that needed stock tips, investments, and more. This time I wouldn't get caught! I would even set up a new website and make sure no one traced it back to me or knew it was me.

www.IDidItHa-Ha.com

is now in business, and you can ask me anything.

9 781604 149128